David the Rebel

叛逆大維打工記

Coleen Reddy　著

倪靖、郜欣、王平　繪

蘇秋華　譯

三民書局

In Memory of Pat

The Granny with a dry sense of humor!

謹以此書紀念 Pat——
我那堪稱是冷面笑匠的外婆!

It's tough being thirteen years old. David knew all about that. His big problem was MONEY. He needed money and he needed lots of it. A thirteen-year-old can't survive without money. His parents always said he WANTED money, but that wasn't true. He NEEDED money.

He needed money to buy clothes. His parents bought him clothes, but they bought boring clothes that he was embarrassed to wear. His mom still bought him Pikachu underwear! He also needed money to go to the movies. Right now though, he needed money for something else.

Valentine's Day was next week, and he needed to get a Valentine's gift for Amy Smith. Amy Smith was his friend, and he really liked her. He wanted to buy her a Valentine's Day card, a box of expensive chocolates, and a cute teddy bear. Girls liked that sort of thing. They loved gifts. Amy was sure to love his gifts. Maybe she would even love him a little.

He didn't have any money because he had spent his allowance on a pair of jeans. He had to ask his parents for more money. His father was like Mr. Scrooge. He would have to beg for the money.

"Dad, I need some money," said David.

"You mean that you WANT some money," said his father.

"No, I NEED it for something important," said David.

"What do you need the money for, David?" asked his dad.

8

David couldn't really tell his dad that he needed money to buy Amy a Valentine's gift. That would be too embarrassing and his father wouldn't understand. He would probably say that David was too young to be thinking about girls…blah, blah, blah…

"I just need it, Dad. Come on. You're my father. I'm your son. You're supposed to give me money," said David.

"I'll give you money if you tell me what it's for," said his dad.

"I can't, Dad," said David. It didn't look like his dad was going to give him anything.

"If you can't tell me then I can't give you money. But you can EARN money," said his dad.

"What do you mean?" asked David.

"If you do some work around the house, I could pay you for it," said his dad.

"What do you want me to do?" asked David.

"The living room and the bathroom need to be painted. If you do that, I will pay you $25," said his father.

"Okay, I'll paint it next weekend after you give me the money," said David.

"No, David. Paint the rooms first, then I'll pay you," said his dad firmly.

"But it will take forever," said David.

"That's the only way that you'll get money out of me," said his father.

"That's not fair," said David.

"Take it or leave it," said his father.

David could see that his father meant  what he said. He decided to give it a try.

David put on some old, ugly clothes that he never wore anymore and started painting. He started in the living room. He worked hard. After half an hour, he was finished.

"It wasn't as hard as I thought it would be," thought David.

He called his father to take a look at his hard work. His father and mother walked into the living room. Their smiles dropped off their faces.

"Oh no!" said his mother.

"What have you done?" asked his father angrily.

"I painted the walls like you asked me to do," said David.

"You didn't do a very good job," said his father, "in fact, you've done a terrible job!"

"I don't understand," said David. What was wrong with his parents? They were never satisfied with anything.

"There are three paintings on the wall. You're supposed to remove them before you paint. You can't just paint around them," said his father.

"And you should have taken all the furniture out," said his mom, "you've dropped paint all over my expensive sofas. They're ruined!"

"I'm not paying you for this," said his father, "you have to do it again."

"No way! I am not your slave! I don't want your stupid money," said David angrily. He went to his room and slammed the door. What would he do now?

David had to get a job, but the only job he could get was delivering newspapers. He would have to do it.

The next morning, he started. He had 100 newspapers to deliver. He would use his bicycle. He started a few blocks away from his home. It was hard work.

He was supposed to throw the newspapers from his bicycle to the doorsteps. But David couldn't aim well. The newspapers landed in trees and once it even landed on the roof. But the worst was when he threw a newspaper and it hit an old man in the face. The old man yelled at him.

David stopped throwing newspapers. He got off his bicycle and put each newspaper right at each doorstep. This took a long time. It was so hot that David started sweating. Sweat was pouring down his face, down his back, and even down his legs.

His newspaper route took him to the street that Amy lived on. He hoped she didn't see him because he looked and smelt so bad. He had to deliver a newspaper to the house right next to Amy's house! He got off his bicycle and walked into the yard to deliver the newspaper. He had taken a few steps when he heard a growl. He turned around and saw a dog. It was growling at him and it had big, sharp teeth.

David was afraid of dogs. He started screaming and tried to run away but the dog was too fast. The dog barked loudly. People came out of their houses to see what was going on. Amy and her brother, Jack, also came out to look.

"Isn't that your friend David?" asked Jack.

"Yes, what is he doing?" asked Amy.

"Hey David, cool underpants!" said Jack. Amy giggled. David looked down and groaned. He had forgotten. He was wearing the Pikachu underwear that his mother had bought him. It had been the worst day of his life.

叛逆大維打工記

十三歲的孩子可真不好當，大維可以深切體會這句話的含意。他最大的問題就是：「錢」。他需要錢，很多的錢。一個十三歲的孩子沒有錢是無法生存的，他的爸媽總認為他「想要」錢，但他們錯了，他不是「想要」錢，而是「需要」錢。他需要錢買衣服。爸媽雖然會買衣服給他，可是他們選的都是些醜到讓他覺得穿出去很丟臉的衣服。他都那麼大了，媽媽居然還會買皮卡丘的內褲給他！他還需要錢看電影。而現在他則需要錢買東西——下個禮拜就是情人節了，大維想買個情人節禮物送愛玫‧史密斯。他和愛玫是朋友，而且他很喜歡她，所以他希望能買張情人節卡片、一盒昂貴的巧克力，以及一隻可愛的泰迪熊送她。女生都喜歡這些玩意兒，她們最愛收到禮物了，所以他認為愛玫一定會喜歡他送的禮物，搞不好還會因此而愛上他呢！問題是他已經把全部財產拿去買了一條牛仔褲，所以現在是半毛錢也不剩了。他得再向爸媽要一點錢。他的爸爸是個一毛不拔的鐵公雞，大維知道他非得低聲下氣的才能**ㄠ**得到一點零用錢。

(p.1～p.7)

中英對照

探索英文叢書・中高級

波波 唸翻天系列

你知道可愛的小兔子也會 "碎碎唸" 嗎？

波波就是這樣。

他將要告訴我們什麼有趣的故事呢？

波波的復活節／波波的西部冒險記／波波上課記

我愛你，波波／波波的下雪天／波波郊遊去

波波打球記／聖誕快樂，波波／波波的萬聖夜

共 9 本，每本均附 CD

國家圖書館出版品預行編目資料

David the Rebel:叛逆大維打工記 / Coleen Reddy著;
　倪靖, 郜欣, 王平繪; 蘇秋華譯.－－初版一刷.－－
臺北市; 三民，2002
　　面；公分－－(愛閱雙語叢書. 青春記事簿系列)
中英對照
ISBN 957-14-3660-7　(平裝)

805

© **David the Rebel**
　　──叛逆大維打工記

著作人　Coleen Reddy
繪　圖　倪靖　郜欣　王平
譯　者　蘇秋華
發行人　劉振強
著作財　三民書局股份有限公司
產權人　臺北市復興北路三八六號
發行所　三民書局股份有限公司
　　　　地址／臺北市復興北路三八六號
　　　　電話／二五〇〇六六〇〇
　　　　郵撥／〇〇〇九九九八──五號
印刷所　三民書局股份有限公司
門市部　復北店／臺北市復興北路三八六號
　　　　重南店／臺北市重慶南路一段六十一號
初版一刷　西元二〇〇二年十一月
編　號　S 85621
定　價　新臺幣參佰伍拾元整
行政院新聞局登記證局版臺業字第〇二〇〇號